The Second Book of

SAMUEL

Start Publishing PD LLC

Manufactured in the United States of America

Cover art: Shutterstock/Taisiya Kozorez

Cover design: Jennifer Do

10 9 8 7 6 5 4 3 2 1

ISBN 979-8-8809-1097-7

The Second Book of

SAMUEL

CHAPTER 1

1:1 Now it came to pass after the death of Saul, when David was returned
from the slaughter of the Amalekites, and David had abode two days in
Ziklag; 1:2 It came even to pass on the third day, that, behold, a man came
out of the camp from Saul with his clothes rent, and earth upon his head:
and so it was, when he came to David, that he fell to the earth, and did
obeisance. 1:3 And David said unto him, From whence comest thou? And
he said unto him, Out of the camp of Israel am I escaped. 1:4 And David
said unto him, How went the matter? I pray thee, tell me. And he answered,
That the people are fled from the battle, and many of the people also are
fallen and dead; and Saul and Jonathan his son are dead also. 1:5 And David
said unto the young man that told him, How knowest thou that Saul and
Jonathan his son be dead? 1:6 And the young man that told him said, As I
happened by chance upon mount Gilboa, behold, Saul leaned upon his
spear; and, lo, the chariots and horsemen followed hard after him. 1:7 And
when he looked behind him, he saw me, and called unto me. And I
answered, Here am I. 1:8 And he said unto me, Who art thou? And I
answered him, I am an Amalekite. 1:9 He said unto me again, Stand, I pray
thee, upon me, and slay me: for anguish is come upon me, because my life
is yet whole in me. 1:10 So I stood upon him, and slew him, because I was
sure that he could not live after that he was fallen: and I took the crown that
was upon his head, and the bracelet that was on his arm, and have brought
them hither unto my lord. 1:11 Then David took hold on his clothes, and
rent them; and likewise all the men that were with him: 1:12 And they
mourned, and wept, and fasted until even, for Saul, and for Jonathan his son,
and for the people of the LORD, and for the house of Israel; because they
were fallen by the sword. 1:13 And David said unto the young man that told
him, Whence art thou? And he answered, I am the son of a stranger, an
Amalekite. 1:14 And David said unto him, How wast thou not afraid to
stretch forth thine hand to destroy the LORD's anointed? 1:15 And David
called one of the young men, and said, Go near, and fall upon him. And he
smote him that he died. 1:16 And David said unto him, Thy blood be upon

thy head; for thy mouth hath testified against thee, saying, I have slain the LORD's anointed. 1:17 And David lamented with this lamentation over Saul and over Jonathan his son: 1:18 (Also he bade them teach the children of Judah the use of the bow: behold, it is written in the book of Jasher.) 1:19 The beauty of Israel is slain upon thy high places: how are the mighty fallen! 1:20 Tell it not in Gath, publish it not in the streets of Askelon; lest the daughters of the Philistines rejoice, lest the daughters of the uncircumcised triumph. 1:21 Ye mountains of Gilboa, let there be no dew, neither let there be rain, upon you, nor fields of offerings: for there the shield of the mighty is vilely cast away, the shield of Saul, as though he had not been anointed with oil. 1:22 From the blood of the slain, from the fat of the mighty, the bow of Jonathan turned not back, and the sword of Saul returned not empty. 1:23 Saul and Jonathan were lovely and pleasant in their lives, and in their death they were not divided: they were swifter than eagles, they were stronger than lions. 1:24 Ye daughters of Israel, weep over Saul, who clothed you in scarlet, with other delights, who put on ornaments of gold upon your apparel. 1:25 How are the mighty fallen in the midst of the battle! O Jonathan, thou wast slain in thine high places. 1:26 I am distressed for thee, my brother Jonathan: very pleasant hast thou been unto me: thy love to me was wonderful, passing the love of women. 1:27 How are the mighty fallen, and the weapons of war perished!

CHAPTER 2

2:1 And it came to pass after this, that David enquired of the LORD, saying, Shall I go up into any of the cities of Judah? And the LORD said unto him, Go up. And David said, Whither shall I go up? And he said, Unto Hebron. 2:2 So David went up thither, and his two wives also, Ahinoam the Jezreelitess, and Abigail Nabal's wife the Carmelite. 2:3 And his men that were with him did David bring up, every man with his household: and they dwelt in the cities of Hebron. 2:4 And the men of Judah came, and there they anointed David king over the house of Judah. And they told David, saying, That the men of Jabeshgilead were they that buried Saul. 2:5 And

David sent messengers unto the men of Jabeshgilead, and said unto them, Blessed be ye of the LORD, that ye have shewed this kindness unto your lord, even unto Saul, and have buried him. 2:6 And now the LORD shew kindness and truth unto you: and I also will requite you this kindness, because ye have done this thing. 2:7 Therefore now let your hands be strengthened, and be ye valiant: for your master Saul is dead, and also the house of Judah have anointed me king over them. 2:8 But Abner the son of Ner, captain of Saul's host, took Ishbosheth the son of Saul, and brought him over to Mahanaim; 2:9 And made him king over Gilead, and over the Ashurites, and over Jezreel, and over Ephraim, and over Benjamin, and over all Israel. 2:10 Ishbosheth Saul's son was forty years old when he began to reign over Israel, and reigned two years. But the house of Judah followed David. 2:11 And the time that David was king in Hebron over the house of Judah was seven years and six months. 2:12 And Abner the son of Ner, and the servants of Ishbosheth the son of Saul, went out from Mahanaim to Gibeon. 2:13 And Joab the son of Zeruiah, and the servants of David, went out, and met together by the pool of Gibeon: and they sat down, the one on the one side of the pool, and the other on the other side of the pool. 2:14 And Abner said to Joab, Let the young men now arise, and play before us. And Joab said, Let them arise. 2:15 Then there arose and went over by number twelve of Benjamin, which pertained to Ishbosheth the son of Saul, and twelve of the servants of David. 2:16 And they caught every one his fellow by the head, and thrust his sword in his fellow's side; so they fell down together: wherefore that place was called Helkathhazzurim, which is in Gibeon. 2:17 And there was a very sore battle that day; and Abner was beaten, and the men of Israel, before the servants of David. 2:18 And there were three sons of Zeruiah there, Joab, and Abishai, and Asahel: and Asahel was as light of foot as a wild roe. 2:19 And Asahel pursued after Abner; and in going he turned not to the right hand nor to the left from following Abner. 2:20 Then Abner looked behind him, and said, Art thou Asahel? And he answered, I am. 2:21 And Abner said to him, Turn thee aside to thy right hand or to thy left, and lay thee hold on one of the young men, and

take thee his armour. But Asahel would not turn aside from following of
him. 2:22 And Abner said again to Asahel, Turn thee aside from following
me: wherefore should I smite thee to the ground? how then should I hold up
my face to Joab thy brother? 2:23 Howbeit he refused to turn aside:
wherefore Abner with the hinder end of the spear smote him under the fifth
rib, that the spear came out behind him; and he fell down there, and died in
the same place: and it came to pass, that as many as came to the place where
Asahel fell down and died stood still. 2:24 Joab also and Abishai pursued
after Abner: and the sun went down when they were come to the hill of
Ammah, that lieth before Giah by the way of the wilderness of Gibeon. 2:25
And the children of Benjamin gathered themselves together after Abner, and
became one troop, and stood on the top of an hill. 2:26 Then Abner called
to Joab, and said, Shall the sword devour for ever? knowest thou not that it
will be bitterness in the latter end? how long shall it be then, ere thou bid the
people return from following their brethren? 2:27 And Joab said, As God
liveth, unless thou hadst spoken, surely then in the morning the people had
gone up every one from following his brother. 2:28 So Joab blew a trumpet,
and all the people stood still, and pursued after Israel no more, neither
fought they any more. 2:29 And Abner and his men walked all that night
through the plain, and passed over Jordan, and went through all Bithron,
and they came to Mahanaim. 2:30 And Joab returned from following Abner:
and when he had gathered all the people together, there lacked of David's
servants nineteen men and Asahel. 2:31 But the servants of David had
smitten of Benjamin, and of Abner's men, so that three hundred and
threescore men died. 2:32 And they took up Asahel, and buried him in the
sepulchre of his father, which was in Bethlehem. And Joab and his men went
all night, and they came to Hebron at break of day.

CHAPTER 3

3:1 Now there was long war between the house of Saul and the house of
David: but David waxed stronger and stronger, and the house of Saul waxed
weaker and weaker. 3:2 And unto David were sons born in Hebron: and his

firstborn was Amnon, of Ahinoam the Jezreelitess; 3:3 And his second, Chileab, of Abigail the wife of Nabal the Carmelite; and the third, Absalom the son of Maacah the daughter of Talmai king of Geshur; 3:4 And the fourth, Adonijah the son of Haggith; and the fifth, Shephatiah the son of Abital; 3:5 And the sixth, Ithream, by Eglah David's wife. These were born to David in Hebron. 3:6 And it came to pass, while there was war between the house of Saul and the house of David, that Abner made himself strong for the house of Saul. 3:7 And Saul had a concubine, whose name was Rizpah, the daughter of Aiah: and Ishbosheth said to Abner, Wherefore hast thou gone in unto my father's concubine? 3:8 Then was Abner very wroth for the words of Ishbosheth, and said, Am I a dog's head, which against Judah do shew kindness this day unto the house of Saul thy father, to his brethren, and to his friends, and have not delivered thee into the hand of David, that thou chargest me to day with a fault concerning this woman? 3:9 So do God to Abner, and more also, except, as the LORD hath sworn to David, even so I do to him; 3:10 To translate the kingdom from the house of Saul, and to set up the throne of David over Israel and over Judah, from Dan even to Beersheba. 3:11 And he could not answer Abner a word again, because he feared him. 3:12 And Abner sent messengers to David on his behalf, saying, Whose is the land? saying also, Make thy league with me, and, behold, my hand shall be with thee, to bring about all Israel unto thee. 3:13 And he said, Well; I will make a league with thee: but one thing I require of thee, that is, Thou shalt not see my face, except thou first bring Michal Saul's daughter, when thou comest to see my face. 3:14 And David sent messengers to Ishbosheth Saul's son, saying, Deliver me my wife Michal, which I espoused to me for an hundred foreskins of the Philistines. 3:15 And Ishbosheth sent, and took her from her husband, even from Phaltiel the son of Laish. 3:16 And her husband went with her along weeping behind her to Bahurim. Then said Abner unto him, Go, return. And he returned. 3:17 And Abner had communication with the elders of Israel, saying, Ye sought for David in times past to be king over you: 3:18 Now then do it: for the LORD hath spoken of David, saying, By the hand of my servant David I will

save my people Israel out of the hand of the Philistines, and out of the hand
of all their enemies. 3:19 And Abner also spake in the ears of Benjamin: and
Abner went also to speak in the ears of David in Hebron all that seemed
good to Israel, and that seemed good to the whole house of Benjamin. 3:20
So Abner came to David to Hebron, and twenty men with him. And David
made Abner and the men that were with him a feast. 3:21 And Abner said
unto David, I will arise and go, and will gather all Israel unto my lord the
king, that they may make a league with thee, and that thou mayest reign over
all that thine heart desireth. And David sent Abner away; and he went in
peace. 3:22 And, behold, the servants of David and Joab came from
pursuing a troop, and brought in a great spoil with them: but Abner was not
with David in Hebron; for he had sent him away, and he was gone in peace.
3:23 When Joab and all the host that was with him were come, they told
Joab, saying, Abner the son of Ner came to the king, and he hath sent him
away, and he is gone in peace. 3:24 Then Joab came to the king, and said,
What hast thou done? behold, Abner came unto thee; why is it that thou hast
sent him away, and he is quite gone? 3:25 Thou knowest Abner the son of
Ner, that he came to deceive thee, and to know thy going out and thy coming
in, and to know all that thou doest. 3:26 And when Joab was come out from
David, he sent messengers after Abner, which brought him again from the
well of Sirah: but David knew it not. 3:27 And when Abner was returned to
Hebron, Joab took him aside in the gate to speak with him quietly, and
smote him there under the fifth rib, that he died, for the blood of Asahel his
brother. 3:28 And afterward when David heard it, he said, I and my
kingdom are guiltless before the LORD for ever from the blood of Abner the
son of Ner: 3:29 Let it rest on the head of Joab, and on all his father's house;
and let there not fail from the house of Joab one that hath an issue, or that
is a leper, or that leaneth on a staff, or that falleth on the sword, or that
lacketh bread. 3:30 So Joab, and Abishai his brother slew Abner, because he
had slain their brother Asahel at Gibeon in the battle. 3:31 And David said
to Joab, and to all the people that were with him, Rend your clothes, and gird
you with sackcloth, and mourn before Abner. And king David himself

followed the bier. 3:32 And they buried Abner in Hebron: and the king lifted up his voice, and wept at the grave of Abner; and all the people wept. 3:33 And the king lamented over Abner, and said, Died Abner as a fool dieth? 3:34 Thy hands were not bound, nor thy feet put into fetters: as a man falleth before wicked men, so fellest thou. And all the people wept again over him. 3:35 And when all the people came to cause David to eat meat while it was yet day, David sware, saying, So do God to me, and more also, if I taste bread, or ought else, till the sun be down. 3:36 And all the people took notice of it, and it pleased them: as whatsoever the king did pleased all the people. 3:37 For all the people and all Israel understood that day that it was not of the king to slay Abner the son of Ner. 3:38 And the king said unto his servants, Know ye not that there is a prince and a great man fallen this day in Israel? 3:39 And I am this day weak, though anointed king; and these men the sons of Zeruiah be too hard for me: the LORD shall reward the doer of evil according to his wickedness.

CHAPTER 4

4:1 And when Saul's son heard that Abner was dead in Hebron, his hands were feeble, and all the Israelites were troubled. 4:2 And Saul's son had two men that were captains of bands: the name of the one was Baanah, and the name of the other Rechab, the sons of Rimmon a Beerothite, of the children of Benjamin: (for Beeroth also was reckoned to Benjamin. 4:3 And the Beerothites fled to Gittaim, and were sojourners there until this day.) 4:4 And Jonathan, Saul's son, had a son that was lame of his feet. He was five years old when the tidings came of Saul and Jonathan out of Jezreel, and his nurse took him up, and fled: and it came to pass, as she made haste to flee, that he fell, and became lame. And his name was Mephibosheth. 4:5 And the sons of Rimmon the Beerothite, Rechab and Baanah, went, and came about the heat of the day to the house of Ishbosheth, who lay on a bed at noon. 4:6 And they came thither into the midst of the house, as though they would have fetched wheat; and they smote him under the fifth rib: and Rechab and Baanah his brother escaped. 4:7 For when they came into the

house, he lay on his bed in his bedchamber, and they smote him, and slew
him, and beheaded him, and took his head, and gat them away through the
plain all night. 4:8 And they brought the head of Ishbosheth unto David to
Hebron, and said to the king, Behold the head of Ishbosheth the son of Saul
thine enemy, which sought thy life; and the LORD hath avenged my lord the
king this day of Saul, and of his seed. 4:9 And David answered Rechab and
Baanah his brother, the sons of Rimmon the Beerothite, and said unto them,
As the LORD liveth, who hath redeemed my soul out of all adversity, 4:10
When one told me, saying, Behold, Saul is dead, thinking to have brought
good tidings, I took hold of him, and slew him in Ziklag, who thought that
I would have given him a reward for his tidings: 4:11 How much more, when
wicked men have slain a righteous person in his own house upon his bed?
shall I not therefore now require his blood of your hand, and take you away
from the earth? 4:12 And David commanded his young men, and they slew
them, and cut off their hands and their feet, and hanged them up over the
pool in Hebron. But they took the head of Ishbosheth, and buried it in the
sepulchre of Abner in Hebron.

CHAPTER 5

5:1 Then came all the tribes of Israel to David unto Hebron, and spake,
saying, Behold, we are thy bone and thy flesh. 5:2 Also in time past, when
Saul was king over us, thou wast he that leddest out and broughtest in Israel:
and the LORD said to thee, Thou shalt feed my people Israel, and thou shalt
be a captain over Israel. 5:3 So all the elders of Israel came to the king to
Hebron; and king David made a league with them in Hebron before the
LORD: and they anointed David king over Israel. 5:4 David was thirty years
old when he began to reign, and he reigned forty years. 5:5 In Hebron he
reigned over Judah seven years and six months: and in Jerusalem he reigned
thirty and three years over all Israel and Judah. 5:6 And the king and his
men went to Jerusalem unto the Jebusites, the inhabitants of the land: which
spake unto David, saying, Except thou take away the blind and the lame,
thou shalt not come in hither: thinking, David cannot come in hither. 5:7

Nevertheless David took the strong hold of Zion: the same is the city of David. 5:8 And David said on that day, Whosoever getteth up to the gutter, and smiteth the Jebusites, and the lame and the blind that are hated of David's soul, he shall be chief and captain. Wherefore they said, The blind and the lame shall not come into the house. 5:9 So David dwelt in the fort, and called it the city of David. And David built round about from Millo and inward. 5:10 And David went on, and grew great, and the LORD God of hosts was with him. 5:11 And Hiram king of Tyre sent messengers to David, and cedar trees, and carpenters, and masons: and they built David an house. 5:12 And David perceived that the LORD had established him king over Israel, and that he had exalted his kingdom for his people Israel's sake. 5:13 And David took him more concubines and wives out of Jerusalem, after he was come from Hebron: and there were yet sons and daughters born to David. 5:14 And these be the names of those that were born unto him in Jerusalem; Shammuah, and Shobab, and Nathan, and Solomon, 5:15 Ibhar also, and Elishua, and Nepheg, and Japhia, 5:16 And Elishama, and Eliada, and Eliphalet. 5:17 But when the Philistines heard that they had anointed David king over Israel, all the Philistines came up to seek David; and David heard of it, and went down to the hold. 5:18 The Philistines also came and spread themselves in the valley of Rephaim. 5:19 And David enquired of the LORD, saying, Shall I go up to the Philistines? wilt thou deliver them into mine hand? And the LORD said unto David, Go up: for I will doubtless deliver the Philistines into thine hand. 5:20 And David came to Baalperazim, and David smote them there, and said, The LORD hath broken forth upon mine enemies before me, as the breach of waters. Therefore he called the name of that place Baalperazim. 5:21 And there they left their images, and David and his men burned them. 5:22 And the Philistines came up yet again, and spread themselves in the valley of Rephaim. 5:23 And when David enquired of the LORD, he said, Thou shalt not go up; but fetch a compass behind them, and come upon them over against the mulberry trees. 5:24 And let it be, when thou hearest the sound of a going in the tops of the mulberry trees, that then thou shalt bestir thyself: for then shall the

LORD go out before thee, to smite the host of the Philistines. 5:25 And David did so, as the LORD had commanded him; and smote the Philistines from Geba until thou come to Gazer.

CHAPTER 6

6:1 Again, David gathered together all the chosen men of Israel, thirty thousand. 6:2 And David arose, and went with all the people that were with him from Baale of Judah, to bring up from thence the ark of God, whose name is called by the name of the LORD of hosts that dwelleth between the cherubims. 6:3 And they set the ark of God upon a new cart, and brought it out of the house of Abinadab that was in Gibeah: and Uzzah and Ahio, the sons of Abinadab, drave the new cart. 6:4 And they brought it out of the house of Abinadab which was at Gibeah, accompanying the ark of God: and Ahio went before the ark. 6:5 And David and all the house of Israel played before the LORD on all manner of instruments made of fir wood, even on harps, and on psalteries, and on timbrels, and on cornets, and on cymbals. 6:6 And when they came to Nachon's threshingfloor, Uzzah put forth his hand to the ark of God, and took hold of it; for the oxen shook it. 6:7 And the anger of the LORD was kindled against Uzzah; and God smote him there for his error; and there he died by the ark of God. 6:8 And David was displeased, because the LORD had made a breach upon Uzzah: and he called the name of the place Perezuzzah to this day. 6:9 And David was afraid of the LORD that day, and said, How shall the ark of the LORD come to me? 6:10 So David would not remove the ark of the LORD unto him into the city of David: but David carried it aside into the house of Obededom the Gittite. 6:11 And the ark of the LORD continued in the house of Obededom the Gittite three months: and the LORD blessed Obededom, and all his household. 6:12 And it was told king David, saying, The LORD hath blessed the house of Obededom, and all that pertaineth unto him, because of the ark of God. So David went and brought up the ark of God from the house of Obededom into the city of David with gladness. 6:13 And it was so, that when they that bare the ark of the LORD had gone six paces, he sacrificed oxen and fatlings. 6:14 And David danced before the LORD with all his might; and David was girded with a linen ephod. 6:15 So David and all the house of Israel brought up the ark of the LORD with shouting, and with the sound of the trumpet. 6:16 And as the ark of the LORD came into the city of David, Michal Saul's daughter looked through a window, and saw king David leaping and dancing before the LORD; and she despised him in her heart. 6:17 And they brought in the ark of the LORD, and set it in his place, in the midst of the tabernacle that David had pitched for it: and David offered burnt offerings and peace offerings before the LORD. 6:18 And as soon as David had made an end of offering burnt offerings and peace offerings, he blessed the people in the name of the LORD of hosts. 6:19 And he dealt among all the people, even among the whole multitude of Israel, as well to the women as men, to every one a cake of bread, and a good piece of flesh, and a flagon of wine. So all the people departed every one to his house. 6:20 Then David returned to bless his household. And Michal the daughter of Saul came out to meet David, and said, How glorious was the king of Israel to day, who uncovered himself to day in the eyes of the handmaids of his servants, as one of the vain fellows shamelessly uncovereth himself! 6:21 And David said unto Michal, It was before the LORD, which chose me before thy father, and before all his house, to appoint me ruler over the people of the LORD, over Israel: therefore will I play before the LORD. 6:22 And I will yet be more vile than thus, and will be base in mine own sight: and of the maidservants which thou hast spoken of, of them shall I be had in honour. 6:23 Therefore Michal the daughter of Saul had no child unto the day of her death.

CHAPTER 7

7:1 And it came to pass, when the king sat in his house, and the LORD had given him rest round about from all his enemies; 7:2 That the king said unto Nathan the prophet, See now, I dwell in an house of cedar, but the ark of God dwelleth within curtains. 7:3 And Nathan said to the king, Go, do all that is in thine heart; for the LORD is with thee. 7:4 And it came to pass

that night, that the word of the LORD came unto Nathan, saying, 7:5 Go
and tell my servant David, Thus saith the LORD, Shalt thou build me an
house for me to dwell in? 7:6 Whereas I have not dwelt in any house since
the time that I brought up the children of Israel out of Egypt, even to this
day, but have walked in a tent and in a tabernacle. 7:7 In all the places
wherein I have walked with all the children of Israel spake I a word with any
of the tribes of Israel, whom I commanded to feed my people Israel, saying,
Why build ye not me an house of cedar? 7:8 Now therefore so shalt thou say
unto my servant David, Thus saith the LORD of hosts, I took thee from the
sheepcote, from following the sheep, to be ruler over my people, over Israel:
7:9 And I was with thee whithersoever thou wentest, and have cut off all
thine enemies out of thy sight, and have made thee a great name, like unto
the name of the great men that are in the earth. 7:10 Moreover I will
appoint a place for my people Israel, and will plant them, that they may dwell
in a place of their own, and move no more; neither shall the children of
wickedness afflict them any more, as beforetime, 7:11 And as since the time
that I commanded judges to be over my people Israel, and have caused thee
to rest from all thine enemies. Also the LORD telleth thee that he will make
thee an house. 7:12 And when thy days be fulfilled, and thou shalt sleep
with thy fathers, I will set up thy seed after thee, which shall proceed out of
thy bowels, and I will establish his kingdom. 7:13 He shall build an house
for my name, and I will stablish the throne of his kingdom for ever. 7:14 I
will be his father, and he shall be my son. If he commit iniquity, I will
chasten him with the rod of men, and with the stripes of the children of
men: 7:15 But my mercy shall not depart away from him, as I took it from
Saul, whom I put away before thee. 7:16 And thine house and thy kingdom
shall be established for ever before thee: thy throne shall be established for
ever. 7:17 According to all these words, and according to all this vision, so
did Nathan speak unto David. 7:18 Then went king David in, and sat before
the LORD, and he said, Who am I, O Lord GOD? and what is my house,
that thou hast brought me hitherto? 7:19 And this was yet a small thing in
thy sight, O Lord GOD; but thou hast spoken also of thy servant's house for

a great while to come. And is this the manner of man, O Lord GOD? 7:20
And what can David say more unto thee? for thou, Lord GOD, knowest thy
servant. 7:21 For thy word's sake, and according to thine own heart, hast
thou done all these great things, to make thy servant know them. 7:22
Wherefore thou art great, O LORD God: for there is none like thee, neither
is there any God beside thee, according to all that we have heard with our
ears. 7:23 And what one nation in the earth is like thy people, even like
Israel, whom God went to redeem for a people to himself, and to make him
a name, and to do for you great things and terrible, for thy land, before thy
people, which thou redeemedst to thee from Egypt, from the nations and
their gods? 7:24 For thou hast confirmed to thyself thy people Israel to be a
people unto thee for ever: and thou, LORD, art become their God. 7:25
And now, O LORD God, the word that thou hast spoken concerning thy
servant, and concerning his house, establish it for ever, and do as thou hast
said. 7:26 And let thy name be magnified for ever, saying, The LORD of
hosts is the God over Israel: and let the house of thy servant David be
established before thee. 7:27 For thou, O LORD of hosts, God of Israel, hast
revealed to thy servant, saying, I will build thee an house: therefore hath thy
servant found in his heart to pray this prayer unto thee. 7:28 And now, O
Lord GOD, thou art that God, and thy words be true, and thou hast
promised this goodness unto thy servant: 7:29 Therefore now let it please
thee to bless the house of thy servant, that it may continue for ever before
thee: for thou, O Lord GOD, hast spoken it: and with thy blessing let the
house of thy servant be blessed for ever.

CHAPTER 8

8:1 And after this it came to pass that David smote the Philistines, and
subdued them: and David took Methegammah out of the hand of the
Philistines. 8:2 And he smote Moab, and measured them with a line, casting
them down to the ground; even with two lines measured he to put to death,
and with one full line to keep alive. And so the Moabites became David's
servants, and brought gifts. 8:3 David smote also Hadadezer, the son of

Rehob, king of Zobah, as he went to recover his border at the river
Euphrates. 8:4 And David took from him a thousand chariots, and seven
hundred horsemen, and twenty thousand footmen: and David houghed all
the chariot horses, but reserved of them for an hundred chariots. 8:5 And
when the Syrians of Damascus came to succour Hadadezer king of Zobah,
David slew of the Syrians two and twenty thousand men. 8:6 Then David
put garrisons in Syria of Damascus: and the Syrians became servants to
David, and brought gifts. And the LORD preserved David whithersoever he
went. 8:7 And David took the shields of gold that were on the servants of
Hadadezer, and brought them to Jerusalem. 8:8 And from Betah, and from
Berothai, cities of Hadadezer, king David took exceeding much brass. 8:9
When Toi king of Hamath heard that David had smitten all the host of
Hadadezer, 8:10 Then Toi sent Joram his son unto king David, to salute him,
and to bless him, because he had fought against Hadadezer, and smitten him:
for Hadadezer had wars with Toi. And Joram brought with him vessels of
silver, and vessels of gold, and vessels of brass: 8:11 Which also king David
did dedicate unto the LORD, with the silver and gold that he had dedicated
of all nations which he subdued; 8:12 Of Syria, and of Moab, and of the
children of Ammon, and of the Philistines, and of Amalek, and of the spoil
of Hadadezer, son of Rehob, king of Zobah. 8:13 And David gat him a name
when he returned from smiting of the Syrians in the valley of salt, being
eighteen thousand men. 8:14 And he put garrisons in Edom; throughout all
Edom put he garrisons, and all they of Edom became David's servants. And
the LORD preserved David whithersoever he went. 8:15 And David reigned
over all Israel; and David executed judgment and justice unto all his people.
8:16 And Joab the son of Zeruiah was over the host; and Jehoshaphat the son
of Ahilud was recorder; 8:17 And Zadok the son of Ahitub, and Ahimelech
the son of Abiathar, were the priests; and Seraiah was the scribe; 8:18 And
Benaiah the son of Jehoiada was over both the Cherethites and the
Pelethites; and David's sons were chief rulers.

SAMUEL

CHAPTER 9

9:1 And David said, Is there yet any that is left of the house of Saul, that I
may shew him kindness for Jonathan's sake? 9:2 And there was of the house
of Saul a servant whose name was Ziba. And when they had called him unto
David, the king said unto him, Art thou Ziba? And he said, Thy servant is he.
9:3 And the king said, Is there not yet any of the house of Saul, that I may
shew the kindness of God unto him? And Ziba said unto the king, Jonathan
hath yet a son, which is lame on his feet. 9:4 And the king said unto him,
Where is he? And Ziba said unto the king, Behold, he is in the house of
Machir, the son of Ammiel, in Lodebar. 9:5 Then king David sent, and
fetched him out of the house of Machir, the son of Ammiel, from Lodebar.
9:6 Now when Mephibosheth, the son of Jonathan, the son of Saul, was
come unto David, he fell on his face, and did reverence. And David said,
Mephibosheth. And he answered, Behold thy servant! 9:7 And David said
unto him, Fear not: for I will surely shew thee kindness for Jonathan thy
father's sake, and will restore thee all the land of Saul thy father; and thou
shalt eat bread at my table continually. 9:8 And he bowed himself, and said,
What is thy servant, that thou shouldest look upon such a dead dog as I am?
9:9 Then the king called to Ziba, Saul's servant, and said unto him, I have
given unto thy master's son all that pertained to Saul and to all his house.
9:10 Thou therefore, and thy sons, and thy servants, shall till the land for
him, and thou shalt bring in the fruits, that thy master's son may have food
to eat: but Mephibosheth thy master's son shall eat bread alway at my table.
Now Ziba had fifteen sons and twenty servants. 9:11 Then said Ziba unto the
king, According to all that my lord the king hath commanded his servant, so
shall thy servant do. As for Mephibosheth, said the king, he shall eat at my
table, as one of the king's sons. 9:12 And Mephibosheth had a young son,
whose name was Micha. And all that dwelt in the house of Ziba were servants
unto Mephibosheth. 9:13 So Mephibosheth dwelt in Jerusalem: for he did
eat continually at the king's table; and was lame on both his feet.

CHAPTER 10

10:1 And it came to pass after this, that the king of the children of Ammon died, and Hanun his son reigned in his stead. 10:2 Then said David, I will shew kindness unto Hanun the son of Nahash, as his father shewed kindness unto me. And David sent to comfort him by the hand of his servants for his father. And David's servants came into the land of the children of Ammon. 10:3 And the princes of the children of Ammon said unto Hanun their lord, Thinkest thou that David doth honour thy father, that he hath sent comforters unto thee? hath not David rather sent his servants unto thee, to search the city, and to spy it out, and to overthrow it? 10:4 Wherefore Hanun took David's servants, and shaved off the one half of their beards, and cut off their garments in the middle, even to their buttocks, and sent them away. 10:5 When they told it unto David, he sent to meet them, because the men were greatly ashamed: and the king said, Tarry at Jericho until your beards be grown, and then return. 10:6 And when the children of Ammon saw that they stank before David, the children of Ammon sent and hired the Syrians of Bethrehob and the Syrians of Zoba, twenty thousand footmen, and of king Maacah a thousand men, and of Ishtob twelve thousand men. 10:7 And when David heard of it, he sent Joab, and all the host of the mighty men. 10:8 And the children of Ammon came out, and put the battle in array at the entering in of the gate: and the Syrians of Zoba, and of Rehob, and Ishtob, and Maacah, were by themselves in the field. 10:9 When Joab saw that the front of the battle was against him before and behind, he chose of all the choice men of Israel, and put them in array against the Syrians: 10:10 And the rest of the people he delivered into the hand of Abishai his brother, that he might put them in array against the children of Ammon. 10:11 And he said, If the Syrians be too strong for me, then thou shalt help me: but if the children of Ammon be too strong for thee, then I will come and help thee. 10:12 Be of good courage, and let us play the men for our people, and for the cities of our God: and the LORD do that which seemeth him good. 10:13 And Joab drew nigh, and the people that were with him, unto the battle against the Syrians: and they fled before him. 10:14 And when the children of Ammon saw that the Syrians were fled, then fled they also before Abishai, and entered into the city. So Joab returned from the children of Ammon, and came to Jerusalem. 10:15 And when the Syrians saw that they were smitten before Israel, they gathered themselves together. 10:16 And Hadarezer sent, and brought out the Syrians that were beyond the river: and they came to Helam; and Shobach the captain of the host of Hadarezer went before them. 10:17 And when it was told David, he gathered all Israel together, and passed over Jordan, and came to Helam. And the Syrians set themselves in array against David, and fought with him. 10:18 And the Syrians fled before Israel; and David slew the men of seven hundred chariots of the Syrians, and forty thousand horsemen, and smote Shobach the captain of their host, who died there. 10:19 And when all the kings that were servants to Hadarezer saw that they were smitten before Israel, they made peace with Israel, and served them. So the Syrians feared to help the children of Ammon any more.

CHAPTER 11

11:1 And it came to pass, after the year was expired, at the time when kings go forth to battle, that David sent Joab, and his servants with him, and all Israel; and they destroyed the children of Ammon, and besieged Rabbah. But David tarried still at Jerusalem. 11:2 And it came to pass in an eveningtide, that David arose from off his bed, and walked upon the roof of the king's house: and from the roof he saw a woman washing herself; and the woman was very beautiful to look upon. 11:3 And David sent and enquired after the woman. And one said, Is not this Bathsheba, the daughter of Eliam, the wife of Uriah the Hittite? 11:4 And David sent messengers, and took her; and she came in unto him, and he lay with her; for she was purified from her uncleanness: and she returned unto her house. 11:5 And the woman conceived, and sent and told David, and said, I am with child. 11:6 And David sent to Joab, saying, Send me Uriah the Hittite. And Joab sent Uriah to David. 11:7 And when Uriah was come unto him, David demanded of him how Joab did, and how the people did, and how the war prospered.

11:8 And David said to Uriah, Go down to thy house, and wash thy feet. And Uriah departed out of the king's house, and there followed him a mess of meat from the king. 11:9 But Uriah slept at the door of the king's house with all the servants of his lord, and went not down to his house. 11:10 And when they had told David, saying, Uriah went not down unto his house, David said unto Uriah, Camest thou not from thy journey? why then didst thou not go down unto thine house? 11:11 And Uriah said unto David, The ark, and Israel, and Judah, abide in tents; and my lord Joab, and the servants of my lord, are encamped in the open fields; shall I then go into mine house, to eat and to drink, and to lie with my wife? as thou livest, and as thy soul liveth, I will not do this thing. 11:12 And David said to Uriah, Tarry here to day also, and to morrow I will let thee depart. So Uriah abode in Jerusalem that day, and the morrow. 11:13 And when David had called him, he did eat and drink before him; and he made him drunk: and at even he went out to lie on his bed with the servants of his lord, but went not down to his house. 11:14 And it came to pass in the morning, that David wrote a letter to Joab, and sent it by the hand of Uriah. 11:15 And he wrote in the letter, saying, Set ye Uriah in the forefront of the hottest battle, and retire ye from him, that he may be smitten, and die. 11:16 And it came to pass, when Joab observed the city, that he assigned Uriah unto a place where he knew that valiant men were. 11:17 And the men of the city went out, and fought with Joab: and there fell some of the people of the servants of David; and Uriah the Hittite died also. 11:18 Then Joab sent and told David all the things concerning the war; 11:19 And charged the messenger, saying, When thou hast made an end of telling the matters of the war unto the king, 11:20 And if so be that the king's wrath arise, and he say unto thee, Wherefore approached ye so nigh unto the city when ye did fight? knew ye not that they would shoot from the wall? 11:21 Who smote Abimelech the son of Jerubbesheth? did not a woman cast a piece of a millstone upon him from the wall, that he died in Thebez? why went ye nigh the wall? then say thou, Thy servant Uriah the Hittite is dead also. 11:22 So the messenger went, and came and shewed David all that Joab had sent him for. 11:23 And the messenger said unto David, Surely the men prevailed against us, and came out unto us into the field, and we were upon them even unto the entering of the gate. 11:24 And the shooters shot from off the wall upon thy servants; and some of the king's servants be dead, and thy servant Uriah the Hittite is dead also. 11:25 Then David said unto the messenger, Thus shalt thou say unto Joab, Let not this thing displease thee, for the sword devoureth one as well as another: make thy battle more strong against the city, and overthrow it: and encourage thou him. 11:26 And when the wife of Uriah heard that Uriah her husband was dead, she mourned for her husband. 11:27 And when the mourning was past, David sent and fetched her to his house, and she became his wife, and bare him a son. But the thing that David had done displeased the LORD.

CHAPTER 12

12:1 And the LORD sent Nathan unto David. And he came unto him, and said unto him, There were two men in one city; the one rich, and the other poor. 12:2 The rich man had exceeding many flocks and herds: 12:3 But the poor man had nothing, save one little ewe lamb, which he had bought and nourished up: and it grew up together with him, and with his children; it did eat of his own meat, and drank of his own cup, and lay in his bosom, and was unto him as a daughter. 12:4 And there came a traveller unto the rich man, and he spared to take of his own flock and of his own herd, to dress for the wayfaring man that was come unto him; but took the poor man's lamb, and dressed it for the man that was come to him. 12:5 And David's anger was greatly kindled against the man; and he said to Nathan, As the LORD liveth, the man that hath done this thing shall surely die: 12:6 And he shall restore the lamb fourfold, because he did this thing, and because he had no pity. 12:7 And Nathan said to David, Thou art the man. Thus saith the LORD God of Israel, I anointed thee king over Israel, and I delivered thee out of the hand of Saul; 12:8 And I gave thee thy master's house, and thy master's wives into thy bosom, and gave thee the house of Israel and of Judah; and if that had been too little, I would moreover have given unto thee such and such

things. 12:9 Wherefore hast thou despised the commandment of the LORD,
to do evil in his sight? thou hast killed Uriah the Hittite with the sword, and
hast taken his wife to be thy wife, and hast slain him with the sword of the
children of Ammon. 12:10 Now therefore the sword shall never depart from
thine house; because thou hast despised me, and hast taken the wife of Uriah
the Hittite to be thy wife. 12:11 Thus saith the LORD, Behold, I will raise
up evil against thee out of thine own house, and I will take thy wives before
thine eyes, and give them unto thy neighbour, and he shall lie with thy wives
in the sight of this sun. 12:12 For thou didst it secretly: but I will do this
thing before all Israel, and before the sun. 12:13 And David said unto
Nathan, I have sinned against the LORD. And Nathan said unto David, The
LORD also hath put away thy sin; thou shalt not die. 12:14 Howbeit,
because by this deed thou hast given great occasion to the enemies of the
LORD to blaspheme, the child also that is born unto thee shall surely die.
12:15 And Nathan departed unto his house. And the LORD struck the child
that Uriah's wife bare unto David, and it was very sick. 12:16 David
therefore besought God for the child; and David fasted, and went in, and lay
all night upon the earth. 12:17 And the elders of his house arose, and went
to him, to raise him up from the earth: but he would not, neither did he eat
bread with them. 12:18 And it came to pass on the seventh day, that the
child died. And the servants of David feared to tell him that the child was
dead: for they said, Behold, while the child was yet alive, we spake unto him,
and he would not hearken unto our voice: how will he then vex himself, if
we tell him that the child is dead? 12:19 But when David saw that his
servants whispered, David perceived that the child was dead: therefore David
said unto his servants, Is the child dead? And they said, He is dead. 12:20
Then David arose from the earth, and washed, and anointed himself, and
changed his apparel, and came into the house of the LORD, and
worshipped: then he came to his own house; and when he required, they set
bread before him, and he did eat. 12:21 Then said his servants unto him,
What thing is this that thou hast done? thou didst fast and weep for the
child, while it was alive; but when the child was dead, thou didst rise and eat

bread. 12:22 And he said, While the child was yet alive, I fasted and wept: for I said, Who can tell whether GOD will be gracious to me, that the child may live? 12:23 But now he is dead, wherefore should I fast? can I bring him back again? I shall go to him, but he shall not return to me. 12:24 And David comforted Bathsheba his wife, and went in unto her, and lay with her: and she bare a son, and he called his name Solomon: and the LORD loved him. 12:25 And he sent by the hand of Nathan the prophet; and he called his name Jedidiah, because of the LORD. 12:26 And Joab fought against Rabbah of the children of Ammon, and took the royal city. 12:27 And Joab sent messengers to David, and said, I have fought against Rabbah, and have taken the city of waters. 12:28 Now therefore gather the rest of the people together, and encamp against the city, and take it: lest I take the city, and it be called after my name. 12:29 And David gathered all the people together, and went to Rabbah, and fought against it, and took it. 12:30 And he took their king's crown from off his head, the weight whereof was a talent of gold with the precious stones: and it was set on David's head. And he brought forth the spoil of the city in great abundance. 12:31 And he brought forth the people that were therein, and put them under saws, and under harrows of iron, and under axes of iron, and made them pass through the brick-kiln: and thus did he unto all the cities of the children of Ammon. So David and all the people returned unto Jerusalem.

CHAPTER 13

13:1 And it came to pass after this, that Absalom the son of David had a fair sister, whose name was Tamar; and Amnon the son of David loved her. 13:2 And Amnon was so vexed, that he fell sick for his sister Tamar; for she was a virgin; and Amnon thought it hard for him to do anything to her. 13:3 But Amnon had a friend, whose name was Jonadab, the son of Shimeah David's brother: and Jonadab was a very subtil man. 13:4 And he said unto him, Why art thou, being the king's son, lean from day to day? wilt thou not tell me? And Amnon said unto him, I love Tamar, my brother Absalom's sister. 13:5 And Jonadab said unto him, Lay thee down on thy bed, and make

thyself sick: and when thy father cometh to see thee, say unto him, I pray
thee, let my sister Tamar come, and give me meat, and dress the meat in my
sight, that I may see it, and eat it at her hand. 13:6 So Amnon lay down, and
made himself sick: and when the king was come to see him, Amnon said
unto the king, I pray thee, let Tamar my sister come, and make me a couple
of cakes in my sight, that I may eat at her hand. 13:7 Then David sent home
to Tamar, saying, Go now to thy brother Amnon's house, and dress him
meat. 13:8 So Tamar went to her brother Amnon's house; and he was laid
down. And she took flour, and kneaded it, and made cakes in his sight, and
did bake the cakes. 13:9 And she took a pan, and poured them out before
him; but he refused to eat. And Amnon said, Have out all men from me.
And they went out every man from him. 13:10 And Amnon said unto
Tamar, Bring the meat into the chamber, that I may eat of thine hand. And
Tamar took the cakes which she had made, and brought them into the
chamber to Amnon her brother. 13:11 And when she had brought them
unto him to eat, he took hold of her, and said unto her, Come lie with me,
my sister. 13:12 And she answered him, Nay, my brother, do not force me;
for no such thing ought to be done in Israel: do not thou this folly. 13:13
And I, whither shall I cause my shame to go? and as for thee, thou shalt be
as one of the fools in Israel. Now therefore, I pray thee, speak unto the king;
for he will not withhold me from thee. 13:14 Howbeit he would not hearken
unto her voice: but, being stronger than she, forced her, and lay with her.
13:15 Then Amnon hated her exceedingly; so that the hatred wherewith he
hated her was greater than the love wherewith he had loved her. And Amnon
said unto her, Arise, be gone. 13:16 And she said unto him, There is no
cause: this evil in sending me away is greater than the other that thou didst
unto me. But he would not hearken unto her. 13:17 Then he called his
servant that ministered unto him, and said, Put now this woman out from
me, and bolt the door after her. 13:18 And she had a garment of divers
colours upon her: for with such robes were the king's daughters that were
virgins apparelled. Then his servant brought her out, and bolted the door
after her. 13:19 And Tamar put ashes on her head, and rent her garment of

divers colours that was on her, and laid her hand on her head, and went on crying. 13:20 And Absalom her brother said unto her, Hath Amnon thy brother been with thee? but hold now thy peace, my sister: he is thy brother; regard not this thing. So Tamar remained desolate in her brother Absalom's house. 13:21 But when king David heard of all these things, he was very wroth. 13:22 And Absalom spake unto his brother Amnon neither good nor bad: for Absalom hated Amnon, because he had forced his sister Tamar. 13:23 And it came to pass after two full years, that Absalom had sheepshearers in Baalhazor, which is beside Ephraim: and Absalom invited all the king's sons. 13:24 And Absalom came to the king, and said, Behold now, thy servant hath sheepshearers; let the king, I beseech thee, and his servants go with thy servant. 13:25 And the king said to Absalom, Nay, my son, let us not all now go, lest we be chargeable unto thee. And he pressed him: howbeit he would not go, but blessed him. 13:26 Then said Absalom, If not, I pray thee, let my brother Amnon go with us. And the king said unto him, Why should he go with thee? 13:27 But Absalom pressed him, that he let Amnon and all the king's sons go with him. 13:28 Now Absalom had commanded his servants, saying, Mark ye now when Amnon's heart is merry with wine, and when I say unto you, Smite Amnon; then kill him, fear not: have not I commanded you? be courageous, and be valiant. 13:29 And the servants of Absalom did unto Amnon as Absalom had commanded. Then all the king's sons arose, and every man gat him up upon his mule, and fled. 13:30 And it came to pass, while they were in the way, that tidings came to David, saying, Absalom hath slain all the king's sons, and there is not one of them left. 13:31 Then the king arose, and tare his garments, and lay on the earth; and all his servants stood by with their clothes rent. 13:32 And Jonadab, the son of Shimeah David's brother, answered and said, Let not my lord suppose that they have slain all the young men the king's sons; for Amnon only is dead: for by the appointment of Absalom this hath been determined from the day that he forced his sister Tamar. 13:33 Now therefore let not my lord the king take the thing to his heart, to think that all the king's sons are dead: for Amnon only is dead. 13:34 But Absalom fled.

And the young man that kept the watch lifted up his eyes, and looked, and,
behold, there came much people by the way of the hill side behind him.
13:35 And Jonadab said unto the king, Behold, the king's sons come: as thy
servant said, so it is. 13:36 And it came to pass, as soon as he had made an
end of speaking, that, behold, the king's sons came, and lifted up their voice
and wept: and the king also and all his servants wept very sore. 13:37 But
Absalom fled, and went to Talmai, the son of Ammihud, king of Geshur.
And David mourned for his son every day. 13:38 So Absalom fled, and went
to Geshur, and was there three years. 13:39 And the soul of king David
longed to go forth unto Absalom: for he was comforted concerning Amnon,
seeing he was dead.

CHAPTER 14

14:1 Now Joab the son of Zeruiah perceived that the king's heart was toward
Absalom. 14:2 And Joab sent to Tekoah, and fetched thence a wise woman,
and said unto her, I pray thee, feign thyself to be a mourner, and put on now
mourning apparel, and anoint not thyself with oil, but be as a woman that
had a long time mourned for the dead: 14:3 And come to the king, and
speak on this manner unto him. So Joab put the words in her mouth. 14:4
And when the woman of Tekoah spake to the king, she fell on her face to the
ground, and did obeisance, and said, Help, O king. 14:5 And the king said
unto her, What aileth thee? And she answered, I am indeed a widow woman,
and mine husband is dead. 14:6 And thy handmaid had two sons, and they
two strove together in the field, and there was none to part them, but the one
smote the other, and slew him. 14:7 And, behold, the whole family is risen
against thine handmaid, and they said, Deliver him that smote his brother,
that we may kill him, for the life of his brother whom he slew; and we will
destroy the heir also: and so they shall quench my coal which is left, and shall
not leave to my husband neither name nor remainder upon the earth. 14:8
And the king said unto the woman, Go to thine house, and I will give charge
concerning thee. 14:9 And the woman of Tekoah said unto the king, My
lord, O king, the iniquity be on me, and on my father's house: and the king

and his throne be guiltless. 14:10 And the king said, Whoever saith ought unto thee, bring him to me, and he shall not touch thee any more. 14:11 Then said she, I pray thee, let the king remember the LORD thy God, that thou wouldest not suffer the revengers of blood to destroy any more, lest they destroy my son. And he said, As the LORD liveth, there shall not one hair of thy son fall to the earth. 14:12 Then the woman said, Let thine handmaid, I pray thee, speak one word unto my lord the king. And he said, Say on. 14:13 And the woman said, Wherefore then hast thou thought such a thing against the people of God? for the king doth speak this thing as one which is faulty, in that the king doth not fetch home again his banished. 14:14 For we must needs die, and are as water spilt on the ground, which cannot be gathered up again; neither doth God respect any person: yet doth he devise means, that his banished be not expelled from him. 14:15 Now therefore that I am come to speak of this thing unto my lord the king, it is because the people have made me afraid: and thy handmaid said, I will now speak unto the king; it may be that the king will perform the request of his handmaid. 14:16 For the king will hear, to deliver his handmaid out of the hand of the man that would destroy me and my son together out of the inheritance of God. 14:17 Then thine handmaid said, The word of my lord the king shall now be comfortable: for as an angel of God, so is my lord the king to discern good and bad: therefore the LORD thy God will be with thee. 14:18 Then the king answered and said unto the woman, Hide not from me, I pray thee, the thing that I shall ask thee. And the woman said, Let my lord the king now speak. 14:19 And the king said, Is not the hand of Joab with thee in all this? And the woman answered and said, As thy soul liveth, my lord the king, none can turn to the right hand or to the left from ought that my lord the king hath spoken: for thy servant Joab, he bade me, and he put all these words in the mouth of thine handmaid: 14:20 To fetch about this form of speech hath thy servant Joab done this thing: and my lord is wise, according to the wisdom of an angel of God, to know all things that are in the earth. 14:21 And the king said unto Joab, Behold now, I have done this thing: go therefore, bring the young man Absalom again. 14:22 And Joab fell to the ground on his face, and bowed himself, and thanked the king: and Joab said, To day thy servant knoweth that I have found grace in thy sight, my lord, O king, in that the king hath fulfilled the request of his servant. 14:23 So Joab arose and went to Geshur, and brought Absalom to Jerusalem. 14:24 And the king said, Let him turn to his own house, and let him not see my face. So Absalom returned to his own house, and saw not the king's face. 14:25 But in all Israel there was none to be so much praised as Absalom for his beauty: from the sole of his foot even to the crown of his head there was no blemish in him. 14:26 And when he polled his head, (for it was at every year's end that he polled it: because the hair was heavy on him, therefore he polled it:) he weighed the hair of his head at two hundred shekels after the king's weight. 14:27 And unto Absalom there were born three sons, and one daughter, whose name was Tamar: she was a woman of a fair countenance. 14:28 So Absalom dwelt two full years in Jerusalem, and saw not the king's face. 14:29 Therefore Absalom sent for Joab, to have sent him to the king; but he would not come to him: and when he sent again the second time, he would not come. 14:30 Therefore he said unto his servants, See, Joab's field is near mine, and he hath barley there; go and set it on fire. And Absalom's servants set the field on fire. 14:31 Then Joab arose, and came to Absalom unto his house, and said unto him, Wherefore have thy servants set my field on fire? 14:32 And Absalom answered Joab, Behold, I sent unto thee, saying, Come hither, that I may send thee to the king, to say, Wherefore am I come from Geshur? it had been good for me to have been there still: now therefore let me see the king's face; and if there be any iniquity in me, let him kill me. 14:33 So Joab came to the king, and told him: and when he had called for Absalom, he came to the king, and bowed himself on his face to the ground before the king: and the king kissed Absalom.

CHAPTER 15

15:1 And it came to pass after this, that Absalom prepared him chariots and horses, and fifty men to run before him. 15:2 And Absalom rose up early, and stood beside the way of the gate: and it was so, that when any man that had a controversy came to the king for judgment, then Absalom called unto him, and said, Of what city art thou? And he said, Thy servant is of one of the tribes of Israel. 15:3 And Absalom said unto him, See, thy matters are good and right; but there is no man deputed of the king to hear thee. 15:4 Absalom said moreover, Oh that I were made judge in the land, that every man which hath any suit or cause might come unto me, and I would do him justice! 15:5 And it was so, that when any man came nigh to him to do him obeisance, he put forth his hand, and took him, and kissed him. 15:6 And on this manner did Absalom to all Israel that came to the king for judgment: so Absalom stole the hearts of the men of Israel. 15:7 And it came to pass after forty years, that Absalom said unto the king, I pray thee, let me go and pay my vow, which I have vowed unto the LORD, in Hebron. 15:8 For thy servant vowed a vow while I abode at Geshur in Syria, saying, If the LORD shall bring me again indeed to Jerusalem, then I will serve the LORD. 15:9 And the king said unto him, Go in peace. So he arose, and went to Hebron. 15:10 But Absalom sent spies throughout all the tribes of Israel, saying, As soon as ye hear the sound of the trumpet, then ye shall say, Absalom reigneth in Hebron. 15:11 And with Absalom went two hundred men out of Jerusalem, that were called; and they went in their simplicity, and they knew not any thing. 15:12 And Absalom sent for Ahithophel the Gilonite, David's counsellor, from his city, even from Giloh, while he offered sacrifices. And the conspiracy was strong; for the people increased continually with Absalom. 15:13 And there came a messenger to David, saying, The hearts of the men of Israel are after Absalom. 15:14 And David said unto all his servants that were with him at Jerusalem, Arise, and let us flee; for we shall not else escape from Absalom: make speed to depart, lest he overtake us suddenly, and bring evil upon us, and smite the city with the edge of the sword. 15:15 And the king's servants said unto the king, Behold, thy servants are ready to do whatsoever my lord the king shall appoint. 15:16 And the king went forth, and all his household after him. And the king left ten women, which were concubines, to keep the house. 15:17 And the king went forth, and all the people after him, and tarried in a place that was far off. 15:18 And all his servants passed on beside him; and all the Cherethites, and all the Pelethites, and all the Gittites, six hundred men which came after him from Gath, passed on before the king. 15:19 Then said the king to Ittai the Gittite, Wherefore goest thou also with us? return to thy place, and abide with the king: for thou art a stranger, and also an exile. 15:20 Whereas thou camest but yesterday, should I this day make thee go up and down with us? seeing I go whither I may, return thou, and take back thy brethren: mercy and truth be with thee. 15:21 And Ittai answered the king, and said, As the LORD liveth, and as my lord the king liveth, surely in what place my lord the king shall be, whether in death or life, even there also will thy servant be. 15:22 And David said to Ittai, Go and pass over. And Ittai the Gittite passed over, and all his men, and all the little ones that were with him. 15:23 And all the country wept with a loud voice, and all the people passed over: the king also himself passed over the brook Kidron, and all the people passed over, toward the way of the wilderness. 15:24 And lo Zadok also, and all the Levites were with him, bearing the ark of the covenant of God: and they set down the ark of God; and Abiathar went up, until all the people had done passing out of the city. 15:25 And the king said unto Zadok, Carry back the ark of God into the city: if I shall find favour in the eyes of the LORD, he will bring me again, and shew me both it, and his habitation: 15:26 But if he thus say, I have no delight in thee; behold, here am I, let him do to me as seemeth good unto him. 15:27 The king said also unto Zadok the priest, Art not thou a seer? return into the city in peace, and your two sons with you, Ahimaaz thy son, and Jonathan the son of Abiathar. 15:28 See, I will tarry in the plain of the wilderness, until there come word from you to certify me. 15:29 Zadok therefore and Abiathar carried the ark of God again to Jerusalem: and they tarried there. 15:30 And David went up by the ascent of mount Olivet, and wept as he went up, and had his head covered, and he went barefoot: and all the people that was with him covered every man his head, and they went up, weeping as they went up. 15:31 And one told David, saying, Ahithophel is among the conspirators with Absalom. And David said, O LORD, I pray thee, turn the counsel of Ahithophel into foolishness. 15:32 And it came to pass, that when David was come to the top of the mount, where he worshipped God, behold, Hushai the Archite came to meet him with his coat rent, and earth upon his head: 15:33 Unto whom David said, If thou passest on with me, then thou shalt be a burden unto me: 15:34 But if thou return to the city, and say unto Absalom, I will be thy servant, O king; as I have been thy father's servant hitherto, so will I now also be thy servant: then mayest thou for me defeat the counsel of Ahithophel. 15:35 And hast thou not there with thee Zadok and Abiathar the priests? therefore it shall be, that what thing soever thou shalt hear out of the king's house, thou shalt tell it to Zadok and Abiathar the priests. 15:36 Behold, they have there with them their two sons, Ahimaaz Zadok's son, and Jonathan Abiathar's son; and by them ye shall send unto me every thing that ye can hear. 15:37 So Hushai David's friend came into the city, and Absalom came into Jerusalem.

CHAPTER 16

16:1 And when David was a little past the top of the hill, behold, Ziba the servant of Mephibosheth met him, with a couple of asses saddled, and upon them two hundred loaves of bread, and an hundred bunches of raisins, and an hundred of summer fruits, and a bottle of wine. 16:2 And the king said unto Ziba, What meanest thou by these? And Ziba said, The asses be for the king's household to ride on; and the bread and summer fruit for the young men to eat; and the wine, that such as be faint in the wilderness may drink. 16:3 And the king said, And where is thy master's son? And Ziba said unto the king, Behold, he abideth at Jerusalem: for he said, To day shall the house of Israel restore me the kingdom of my father. 16:4 Then said the king to Ziba, Behold, thine are all that pertained unto Mephibosheth. And Ziba said, I humbly beseech thee that I may find grace in thy sight, my lord, O king. 16:5 And when king David came to Bahurim, behold, thence came out a man of the family of the house of Saul, whose name was Shimei, the son of Gera: he came forth, and cursed still as he came. 16:6 And he cast stones at David, and at all the servants of king David: and all the people and all the mighty men were on his right hand and on his left. 16:7 And thus said

Shimei when he cursed, Come out, come out, thou bloody man, and thou man of Belial: 16:8 The LORD hath returned upon thee all the blood of the house of Saul, in whose stead thou hast reigned; and the LORD hath delivered the kingdom into the hand of Absalom thy son: and, behold, thou art taken in thy mischief, because thou art a bloody man. 16:9 Then said Abishai the son of Zeruiah unto the king, Why should this dead dog curse my lord the king? let me go over, I pray thee, and take off his head. 16:10 And the king said, What have I to do with you, ye sons of Zeruiah? so let him curse, because the LORD hath said unto him, Curse David. Who shall then say, Wherefore hast thou done so? 16:11 And David said to Abishai, and to all his servants, Behold, my son, which came forth of my bowels, seeketh my life: how much more now may this Benjamite do it? let him alone, and let him curse; for the LORD hath bidden him. 16:12 It may be that the LORD will look on mine affliction, and that the LORD will requite me good for his cursing this day. 16:13 And as David and his men went by the way, Shimei went along on the hill's side over against him, and cursed as he went, and threw stones at him, and cast dust. 16:14 And the king, and all the people that were with him, came weary, and refreshed themselves there. 16:15 And Absalom, and all the people the men of Israel, came to Jerusalem, and Ahithophel with him. 16:16 And it came to pass, when Hushai the Archite, David's friend, was come unto Absalom, that Hushai said unto Absalom, God save the king, God save the king. 16:17 And Absalom said to Hushai, Is this thy kindness to thy friend? why wentest thou not with thy friend? 16:18 And Hushai said unto Absalom, Nay; but whom the LORD, and this people, and all the men of Israel, choose, his will I be, and with him will I abide. 16:19 And again, whom should I serve? should I not serve in the presence of his son? as I have served in thy father's presence, so will I be in thy presence. 16:20 Then said Absalom to Ahithophel, Give counsel among you what we shall do. 16:21 And Ahithophel said unto Absalom, Go in unto thy father's concubines, which he hath left to keep the house; and all Israel shall hear that thou art abhorred of thy father: then shall the hands of all that are with thee be strong. 16:22 So they spread Absalom a tent upon the top of the house; and Absalom went in unto his father's concubines in the sight of all Israel. 16:23 And the counsel of Ahithophel, which he counselled in those days, was as if a man had enquired at the oracle of God: so was all the counsel of Ahithophel both with David and with Absalom.

CHAPTER 17

17:1 Moreover Ahithophel said unto Absalom, Let me now choose out twelve thousand men, and I will arise and pursue after David this night: 17:2 And I will come upon him while he is weary and weak handed, and will make him afraid: and all the people that are with him shall flee; and I will smite the king only: 17:3 And I will bring back all the people unto thee: the man whom thou seekest is as if all returned: so all the people shall be in peace. 17:4 And the saying pleased Absalom well, and all the elders of Israel. 17:5 Then said Absalom, Call now Hushai the Archite also, and let us hear likewise what he saith. 17:6 And when Hushai was come to Absalom, Absalom spake unto him, saying, Ahithophel hath spoken after this manner: shall we do after his saying? if not; speak thou. 17:7 And Hushai said unto Absalom, The counsel that Ahithophel hath given is not good at this time. 17:8 For, said Hushai, thou knowest thy father and his men, that they be mighty men, and they be chafed in their minds, as a bear robbed of her whelps in the field: and thy father is a man of war, and will not lodge with the people. 17:9 Behold, he is hid now in some pit, or in some other place: and it will come to pass, when some of them be overthrown at the first, that whosoever heareth it will say, There is a slaughter among the people that follow Absalom. 17:10 And he also that is valiant, whose heart is as the heart of a lion, shall utterly melt: for all Israel knoweth that thy father is a mighty man, and they which be with him are valiant men. 17:11 Therefore I counsel that all Israel be generally gathered unto thee, from Dan even to Beersheba, as the sand that is by the sea for multitude; and that thou go to battle in thine own person. 17:12 So shall we come upon him in some place where he shall be found, and we will light upon him as the dew falleth on the ground: and of him and of all the men that are with him there shall not be left so much as one. 17:13

Moreover, if he be gotten into a city, then shall all Israel bring ropes to that city, and we will draw it into the river, until there be not one small stone found there. 17:14 And Absalom and all the men of Israel said, The counsel of Hushai the Archite is better than the counsel of Ahithophel. For the LORD had appointed to defeat the good counsel of Ahithophel, to the intent that the LORD might bring evil upon Absalom. 17:15 Then said Hushai unto Zadok and to Abiathar the priests, Thus and thus did Ahithophel counsel Absalom and the elders of Israel; and thus and thus have I counselled. 17:16 Now therefore send quickly, and tell David, saying, Lodge not this night in the plains of the wilderness, but speedily pass over; lest the king be swallowed up, and all the people that are with him. 17:17 Now Jonathan and Ahimaaz stayed by Enrogel; for they might not be seen to come into the city: and a wench went and told them; and they went and told king David. 17:18 Nevertheless a lad saw them, and told Absalom: but they went both of them away quickly, and came to a man's house in Bahurim, which had a well in his court; whither they went down. 17:19 And the woman took and spread a covering over the well's mouth, and spread ground corn thereon; and the thing was not known. 17:20 And when Absalom's servants came to the woman to the house, they said, Where is Ahimaaz and Jonathan? And the woman said unto them, They be gone over the brook of water. And when they had sought and could not find them, they returned to Jerusalem. 17:21 And it came to pass, after they were departed, that they came up out of the well, and went and told king David, and said unto David, Arise, and pass quickly over the water: for thus hath Ahithophel counselled against you. 17:22 Then David arose, and all the people that were with him, and they passed over Jordan: by the morning light there lacked not one of them that was not gone over Jordan. 17:23 And when Ahithophel saw that his counsel was not followed, he saddled his ass, and arose, and gat him home to his house, to his city, and put his household in order, and hanged himself, and died, and was buried in the sepulchre of his father. 17:24 Then David came to Mahanaim. And Absalom passed over Jordan, he and all the men of Israel with him. 17:25 And Absalom made Amasa captain of the host instead of Joab: which Amasa was a man's son, whose name was Ithra an Israelite, that went in to Abigail the daughter of Nahash, sister to Zeruiah Joab's mother. 17:26 So Israel and Absalom pitched in the land of Gilead. 17:27 And it came to pass, when David was come to Mahanaim, that Shobi the son of Nahash of Rabbah of the children of Ammon, and Machir the son of Ammiel of Lodebar, and Barzillai the Gileadite of Rogelim, 17:28 Brought beds, and basons, and earthen vessels, and wheat, and barley, and flour, and parched corn, and beans, and lentiles, and parched pulse, 17:29 And honey, and butter, and sheep, and cheese of kine, for David, and for the people that were with him, to eat: for they said, The people is hungry, and weary, and thirsty, in the wilderness.

CHAPTER 18

18:1 And David numbered the people that were with him, and set captains of thousands, and captains of hundreds over them. 18:2 And David sent forth a third part of the people under the hand of Joab, and a third part under the hand of Abishai the son of Zeruiah, Joab's brother, and a third part under the hand of Ittai the Gittite. And the king said unto the people, I will surely go forth with you myself also. 18:3 But the people answered, Thou shalt not go forth: for if we flee away, they will not care for us; neither if half of us die, will they care for us: but now thou art worth ten thousand of us: therefore now it is better that thou succour us out of the city. 18:4 And the king said unto them, What seemeth you best I will do. And the king stood by the gate side, and all the people came out by hundreds and by thousands. 18:5 And the king commanded Joab and Abishai and Ittai, saying, Deal gently for my sake with the young man, even with Absalom. And all the people heard when the king gave all the captains charge concerning Absalom. 18:6 So the people went out into the field against Israel: and the battle was in the wood of Ephraim; 18:7 Where the people of Israel were slain before the servants of David, and there was there a great slaughter that day of twenty thousand men. 18:8 For the battle was there scattered over the face of all the country: and the wood devoured more people that day than the

sword devoured. 18:9 And Absalom met the servants of David. And
Absalom rode upon a mule, and the mule went under the thick boughs of a
great oak, and his head caught hold of the oak, and he was taken up between
the heaven and the earth; and the mule that was under him went away.
18:10 And a certain man saw it, and told Joab, and said, Behold, I saw
Absalom hanged in an oak. 18:11 And Joab said unto the man that told
him, And, behold, thou sawest him, and why didst thou not smite him there
to the ground? and I would have given thee ten shekels of silver, and a girdle.
18:12 And the man said unto Joab, Though I should receive a thousand
shekels of silver in mine hand, yet would I not put forth mine hand against
the king's son: for in our hearing the king charged thee and Abishai and Ittai,
saying, Beware that none touch the young man Absalom. 18:13 Otherwise
I should have wrought falsehood against mine own life: for there is no matter
hid from the king, and thou thyself wouldest have set thyself against me.
18:14 Then said Joab, I may not tarry thus with thee. And he took three darts
in his hand, and thrust them through the heart of Absalom, while he was yet
alive in the midst of the oak. 18:15 And ten young men that bare Joab's
armour compassed about and smote Absalom, and slew him. 18:16 And
Joab blew the trumpet, and the people returned from pursuing after Israel:
for Joab held back the people. 18:17 And they took Absalom, and cast him
into a great pit in the wood, and laid a very great heap of stones upon him:
and all Israel fled every one to his tent. 18:18 Now Absalom in his lifetime
had taken and reared up for himself a pillar, which is in the king's dale: for
he said, I have no son to keep my name in remembrance: and he called the
pillar after his own name: and it is called unto this day, Absalom's place.
18:19 Then said Ahimaaz the son of Zadok, Let me now run, and bear the
king tidings, how that the LORD hath avenged him of his enemies. 18:20
And Joab said unto him, Thou shalt not bear tidings this day, but thou shalt
bear tidings another day: but this day thou shalt bear no tidings, because the
king's son is dead. 18:21 Then said Joab to Cushi, Go tell the king what
thou hast seen. And Cushi bowed himself unto Joab, and ran. 18:22 Then
said Ahimaaz the son of Zadok yet again to Joab, But howsoever, let me, I

pray thee, also run after Cushi. And Joab said, Wherefore wilt thou run, my son, seeing that thou hast no tidings ready? 18:23 But howsoever, said he, let me run. And he said unto him, Run. Then Ahimaaz ran by the way of the plain, and overran Cushi. 18:24 And David sat between the two gates: and the watchman went up to the roof over the gate unto the wall, and lifted up his eyes, and looked, and behold a man running alone. 18:25 And the watchman cried, and told the king. And the king said, If he be alone, there is tidings in his mouth. And he came apace, and drew near. 18:26 And the watchman saw another man running: and the watchman called unto the porter, and said, Behold another man running alone. And the king said, He also bringeth tidings. 18:27 And the watchman said, Me thinketh the running of the foremost is like the running of Ahimaaz the son of Zadok. And the king said, He is a good man, and cometh with good tidings. 18:28 And Ahimaaz called, and said unto the king, All is well. And he fell down to the earth upon his face before the king, and said, Blessed be the LORD thy God, which hath delivered up the men that lifted up their hand against my lord the king. 18:29 And the king said, Is the young man Absalom safe? And Ahimaaz answered, When Joab sent the king's servant, and me thy servant, I saw a great tumult, but I knew not what it was. 18:30 And the king said unto him, Turn aside, and stand here. And he turned aside, and stood still. 18:31 And, behold, Cushi came; and Cushi said, Tidings, my lord the king: for the LORD hath avenged thee this day of all them that rose up against thee. 18:32 And the king said unto Cushi, Is the young man Absalom safe? And Cushi answered, The enemies of my lord the king, and all that rise against thee to do thee hurt, be as that young man is. 18:33 And the king was much moved, and went up to the chamber over the gate, and wept: and as he went, thus he said, O my son Absalom, my son, my son Absalom! would God I had died for thee, O Absalom, my son, my son!

CHAPTER 19

19:1 And it was told Joab, Behold, the king weepeth and mourneth for Absalom. 19:2 And the victory that day was turned into mourning unto all

the people: for the people heard say that day how the king was grieved for his
son. 19:3 And the people gat them by stealth that day into the city, as people
being ashamed steal away when they flee in battle. 19:4 But the king covered
his face, and the king cried with a loud voice, O my son Absalom, O
Absalom, my son, my son! 19:5 And Joab came into the house to the king,
and said, Thou hast shamed this day the faces of all thy servants, which this
day have saved thy life, and the lives of thy sons and of thy daughters, and the
lives of thy wives, and the lives of thy concubines; 19:6 In that thou lovest
thine enemies, and hatest thy friends. For thou hast declared this day, that
thou regardest neither princes nor servants: for this day I perceive, that if
Absalom had lived, and all we had died this day, then it had pleased thee
well. 19:7 Now therefore arise, go forth, and speak comfortably unto thy
servants: for I swear by the LORD, if thou go not forth, there will not tarry
one with thee this night: and that will be worse unto thee than all the evil
that befell thee from thy youth until now. 19:8 Then the king arose, and sat
in the gate. And they told unto all the people, saying, Behold, the king doth
sit in the gate. And all the people came before the king: for Israel had fled
every man to his tent. 19:9 And all the people were at strife throughout all
the tribes of Israel, saying, The king saved us out of the hand of our enemies,
and he delivered us out of the hand of the Philistines; and now he is fled out
of the land for Absalom. 19:10 And Absalom, whom we anointed over us,
is dead in battle. Now therefore why speak ye not a word of bringing the king
back? 19:11 And king David sent to Zadok and to Abiathar the priests,
saying, Speak unto the elders of Judah, saying, Why are ye the last to bring
the king back to his house? seeing the speech of all Israel is come to the king,
even to his house. 19:12 Ye are my brethren, ye are my bones and my flesh:
wherefore then are ye the last to bring back the king? 19:13 And say ye to
Amasa, Art thou not of my bone, and of my flesh? God do so to me, and
more also, if thou be not captain of the host before me continually in the
room of Joab. 19:14 And he bowed the heart of all the men of Judah, even
as the heart of one man; so that they sent this word unto the king, Return
thou, and all thy servants. 19:15 So the king returned, and came to Jordan.

And Judah came to Gilgal, to go to meet the king, to conduct the king over
Jordan. 19:16 And Shimei the son of Gera, a Benjamite, which was of
Bahurim, hasted and came down with the men of Judah to meet king David.
19:17 And there were a thousand men of Benjamin with him, and Ziba the
servant of the house of Saul, and his fifteen sons and his twenty servants with
him; and they went over Jordan before the king. 19:18 And there went over
a ferry boat to carry over the king's household, and to do what he thought
good. And Shimei the son of Gera fell down before the king, as he was come
over Jordan; 19:19 And said unto the king, Let not my lord impute iniquity
unto me, neither do thou remember that which thy servant did perversely the
day that my lord the king went out of Jerusalem, that the king should take it
to his heart. 19:20 For thy servant doth know that I have sinned: therefore,
behold, I am come the first this day of all the house of Joseph to go down to
meet my lord the king. 19:21 But Abishai the son of Zeruiah answered and
said, Shall not Shimei be put to death for this, because he cursed the LORD's
anointed? 19:22 And David said, What have I to do with you, ye sons of
Zeruiah, that ye should this day be adversaries unto me? shall there any man
be put to death this day in Israel? for do not I know that I am this day king
over Israel? 19:23 Therefore the king said unto Shimei, Thou shalt not die.
And the king sware unto him. 19:24 And Mephibosheth the son of Saul
came down to meet the king, and had neither dressed his feet, nor trimmed
his beard, nor washed his clothes, from the day the king departed until the
day he came again in peace. 19:25 And it came to pass, when he was come
to Jerusalem to meet the king, that the king said unto him, Wherefore
wentest not thou with me, Mephibosheth? 19:26 And he answered, My lord,
O king, my servant deceived me: for thy servant said, I will saddle me an ass,
that I may ride thereon, and go to the king; because thy servant is lame.
19:27 And he hath slandered thy servant unto my lord the king; but my lord
the king is as an angel of God: do therefore what is good in thine eyes. 19:28
For all of my father's house were but dead men before my lord the king: yet
didst thou set thy servant among them that did eat at thine own table. What
right therefore have I yet to cry any more unto the king? 19:29 And the king

said unto him, Why speakest thou any more of thy matters? I have said, Thou and Ziba divide the land. 19:30 And Mephibosheth said unto the king, Yea, let him take all, forasmuch as my lord the king is come again in peace unto his own house. 19:31 And Barzillai the Gileadite came down from Rogelim, and went over Jordan with the king, to conduct him over Jordan. 19:32 Now Barzillai was a very aged man, even fourscore years old: and he had provided the king of sustenance while he lay at Mahanaim; for he was a very great man. 19:33 And the king said unto Barzillai, Come thou over with me, and I will feed thee with me in Jerusalem. 19:34 And Barzillai said unto the king, How long have I to live, that I should go up with the king unto Jerusalem? 19:35 I am this day fourscore years old: and can I discern between good and evil? can thy servant taste what I eat or what I drink? can I hear any more the voice of singing men and singing women? wherefore then should thy servant be yet a burden unto my lord the king? 19:36 Thy servant will go a little way over Jordan with the king: and why should the king recompense it me with such a reward? 19:37 Let thy servant, I pray thee, turn back again, that I may die in mine own city, and be buried by the grave of my father and of my mother. But behold thy servant Chimham; let him go over with my lord the king; and do to him what shall seem good unto thee. 19:38 And the king answered, Chimham shall go over with me, and I will do to him that which shall seem good unto thee: and whatsoever thou shalt require of me, that will I do for thee. 19:39 And all the people went over Jordan. And when the king was come over, the king kissed Barzillai, and blessed him; and he returned unto his own place. 19:40 Then the king went on to Gilgal, and Chimham went on with him: and all the people of Judah conducted the king, and also half the people of Israel. 19:41 And, behold, all the men of Israel came to the king, and said unto the king, Why have our brethren the men of Judah stolen thee away, and have brought the king, and his household, and all David's men with him, over Jordan? 19:42 And all the men of Judah answered the men of Israel, Because the king is near of kin to us: wherefore then be ye angry for this matter? have we eaten at all of the king's cost? or hath he given us any gift? 19:43 And the men of Israel answered the men of

Judah, and said, We have ten parts in the king, and we have also more right in David than ye: why then did ye despise us, that our advice should not be first had in bringing back our king? And the words of the men of Judah were fiercer than the words of the men of Israel.

CHAPTER 20

20:1 And there happened to be there a man of Belial, whose name was Sheba, the son of Bichri, a Benjamite: and he blew a trumpet, and said, We have no part in David, neither have we inheritance in the son of Jesse: every man to his tents, O Israel. 20:2 So every man of Israel went up from after David, and followed Sheba the son of Bichri: but the men of Judah clave unto their king, from Jordan even to Jerusalem. 20:3 And David came to his house at Jerusalem; and the king took the ten women his concubines, whom he had left to keep the house, and put them in ward, and fed them, but went not in unto them. So they were shut up unto the day of their death, living in widowhood. 20:4 Then said the king to Amasa, Assemble me the men of Judah within three days, and be thou here present. 20:5 So Amasa went to assemble the men of Judah: but he tarried longer than the set time which he had appointed him. 20:6 And David said to Abishai, Now shall Sheba the son of Bichri do us more harm than did Absalom: take thou thy lord's servants, and pursue after him, lest he get him fenced cities, and escape us. 20:7 And there went out after him Joab's men, and the Cherethites, and the Pelethites, and all the mighty men: and they went out of Jerusalem, to pursue after Sheba the son of Bichri. 20:8 When they were at the great stone which is in Gibeon, Amasa went before them. And Joab's garment that he had put on was girded unto him, and upon it a girdle with a sword fastened upon his loins in the sheath thereof; and as he went forth it fell out. 20:9 And Joab said to Amasa, Art thou in health, my brother? And Joab took Amasa by the beard with the right hand to kiss him. 20:10 But Amasa took no heed to the sword that was in Joab's hand: so he smote him therewith in the fifth rib, and shed out his bowels to the ground, and struck him not again; and he died. So Joab and Abishai his brother pursued after Sheba the son of Bichri. 20:11

And one of Joab's men stood by him, and said, He that favoureth Joab, and he that is for David, let him go after Joab. 20:12 And Amasa wallowed in blood in the midst of the highway. And when the man saw that all the people stood still, he removed Amasa out of the highway into the field, and cast a cloth upon him, when he saw that every one that came by him stood still. 20:13 When he was removed out of the highway, all the people went on after Joab, to pursue after Sheba the son of Bichri. 20:14 And he went through all the tribes of Israel unto Abel, and to Bethmaachah, and all the Berites: and they were gathered together, and went also after him. 20:15 And they came and besieged him in Abel of Bethmaachah, and they cast up a bank against the city, and it stood in the trench: and all the people that were with Joab battered the wall, to throw it down. 20:16 Then cried a wise woman out of the city, Hear, hear; say, I pray you, unto Joab, Come near hither, that I may speak with thee. 20:17 And when he was come near unto her, the woman said, Art thou Joab? And he answered, I am he. Then she said unto him, Hear the words of thine handmaid. And he answered, I do hear. 20:18 Then she spake, saying, They were wont to speak in old time, saying, They shall surely ask counsel at Abel: and so they ended the matter. 20:19 I am one of them that are peaceable and faithful in Israel: thou seekest to destroy a city and a mother in Israel: why wilt thou swallow up the inheritance of the LORD? 20:20 And Joab answered and said, Far be it, far be it from me, that I should swallow up or destroy. 20:21 The matter is not so: but a man of mount Ephraim, Sheba the son of Bichri by name, hath lifted up his hand against the king, even against David: deliver him only, and I will depart from the city. And the woman said unto Joab, Behold, his head shall be thrown to thee over the wall. 20:22 Then the woman went unto all the people in her wisdom. And they cut off the head of Sheba the son of Bichri, and cast it out to Joab. And he blew a trumpet, and they retired from the city, every man to his tent. And Joab returned to Jerusalem unto the king. 20:23 Now Joab was over all the host of Israel: and Benaiah the son of Jehoiada was over the Cherethites and over the Pelethites: 20:24 And Adoram was over the tribute: and Jehoshaphat the son of Ahilud was recorder: 20:25 And Sheva was scribe: and Zadok and Abiathar were the priests: 20:26 And Ira also the Jairite was a chief ruler about David.

CHAPTER 21

21:1 Then there was a famine in the days of David three years, year after year; and David enquired of the LORD. And the LORD answered, It is for Saul, and for his bloody house, because he slew the Gibeonites. 21:2 And the king called the Gibeonites, and said unto them; (now the Gibeonites were not of the children of Israel, but of the remnant of the Amorites; and the children of Israel had sworn unto them: and Saul sought to slay them in his zeal to the children of Israel and Judah.) 21:3 Wherefore David said unto the Gibeonites, What shall I do for you? and wherewith shall I make the atonement, that ye may bless the inheritance of the LORD? 21:4 And the Gibeonites said unto him, We will have no silver nor gold of Saul, nor of his house; neither for us shalt thou kill any man in Israel. And he said, What ye shall say, that will I do for you. 21:5 And they answered the king, The man that consumed us, and that devised against us that we should be destroyed from remaining in any of the coasts of Israel, 21:6 Let seven men of his sons be delivered unto us, and we will hang them up unto the LORD in Gibeah of Saul, whom the LORD did choose. And the king said, I will give them. 21:7 But the king spared Mephibosheth, the son of Jonathan the son of Saul, because of the LORD's oath that was between them, between David and Jonathan the son of Saul. 21:8 But the king took the two sons of Rizpah the daughter of Aiah, whom she bare unto Saul, Armoni and Mephibosheth; and the five sons of Michal the daughter of Saul, whom she brought up for Adriel the son of Barzillai the Meholathite: 21:9 And he delivered them into the hands of the Gibeonites, and they hanged them in the hill before the LORD: and they fell all seven together, and were put to death in the days of harvest, in the first days, in the beginning of barley harvest. 21:10 And Rizpah the daughter of Aiah took sackcloth, and spread it for her upon the rock, from the beginning of harvest until water dropped upon them out of heaven, and suffered neither the birds of the air to rest on them by day, nor the beasts of

the field by night. 21:11 And it was told David what Rizpah the daughter of
Aiah, the concubine of Saul, had done. 21:12 And David went and took the
bones of Saul and the bones of Jonathan his son from the men of
Jabeshgilead, which had stolen them from the street of Bethshan, where the
Philistines had hanged them, when the Philistines had slain Saul in Gilboa:
21:13 And he brought up from thence the bones of Saul and the bones of
Jonathan his son; and they gathered the bones of them that were hanged.
21:14 And the bones of Saul and Jonathan his son buried they in the country
of Benjamin in Zelah, in the sepulchre of Kish his father: and they performed
all that the king commanded. And after that God was intreated for the land.
21:15 Moreover the Philistines had yet war again with Israel; and David went
down, and his servants with him, and fought against the Philistines: and
David waxed faint. 21:16 And Ishbibenob, which was of the sons of the
giant, the weight of whose spear weighed three hundred shekels of brass in
weight, he being girded with a new sword, thought to have slain David.
21:17 But Abishai the son of Zeruiah succoured him, and smote the
Philistine, and killed him. Then the men of David sware unto him, saying,
Thou shalt go no more out with us to battle, that thou quench not the light
of Israel. 21:18 And it came to pass after this, that there was again a battle
with the Philistines at Gob: then Sibbechai the Hushathite slew Saph, which
was of the sons of the giant. 21:19 And there was again a battle in Gob with
the Philistines, where Elhanan the son of Jaareoregim, a Bethlehemite, slew
the brother of Goliath the Gittite, the staff of whose spear was like a weaver's
beam. 21:20 And there was yet a battle in Gath, where was a man of great
stature, that had on every hand six fingers, and on every foot six toes, four
and twenty in number; and he also was born to the giant. 21:21 And when
he defied Israel, Jonathan the son of Shimeah the brother of David slew him.
21:22 These four were born to the giant in Gath, and fell by the hand of
David, and by the hand of his servants.

CHAPTER 22

22:1 And David spake unto the LORD the words of this song in the day that the LORD had delivered him out of the hand of all his enemies, and out of the hand of Saul: 22:2 And he said, The LORD is my rock, and my fortress, and my deliverer; 22:3 The God of my rock; in him will I trust: he is my shield, and the horn of my salvation, my high tower, and my refuge, my saviour; thou savest me from violence. 22:4 I will call on the LORD, who is worthy to be praised: so shall I be saved from mine enemies. 22:5 When the waves of death compassed me, the floods of ungodly men made me afraid; 22:6 The sorrows of hell compassed me about; the snares of death prevented me; 22:7 In my distress I called upon the LORD, and cried to my God: and he did hear my voice out of his temple, and my cry did enter into his ears. 22:8 Then the earth shook and trembled; the foundations of heaven moved and shook, because he was wroth. 22:9 There went up a smoke out of his nostrils, and fire out of his mouth devoured: coals were kindled by it. 22:10 He bowed the heavens also, and came down; and darkness was under his feet. 22:11 And he rode upon a cherub, and did fly: and he was seen upon the wings of the wind. 22:12 And he made darkness pavilions round about him, dark waters, and thick clouds of the skies. 22:13 Through the brightness before him were coals of fire kindled. 22:14 The LORD thundered from heaven, and the most High uttered his voice. 22:15 And he sent out arrows, and scattered them; lightning, and discomfited them. 22:16 And the channels of the sea appeared, the foundations of the world were discovered, at the rebuking of the LORD, at the blast of the breath of his nostrils. 22:17 He sent from above, he took me; he drew me out of many waters; 22:18 He delivered me from my strong enemy, and from them that hated me: for they were too strong for me. 22:19 They prevented me in the day of my calamity: but the LORD was my stay. 22:20 He brought me forth also into a large place: he delivered me, because he delighted in me. 22:21 The LORD rewarded me according to my righteousness: according to the cleanness of my hands hath he recompensed me. 22:22 For I have kept the ways of the LORD, and have not wickedly departed from my God. 22:23 For all his judgments were before me: and as for his statutes, I did not depart from them. 22:24 I was also upright before him, and have kept myself from

mine iniquity. 22:25 Therefore the LORD hath recompensed me according
to my righteousness; according to my cleanness in his eye sight. 22:26 With
the merciful thou wilt shew thyself merciful, and with the upright man thou
wilt shew thyself upright. 22:27 With the pure thou wilt shew thyself pure;
and with the froward thou wilt shew thyself unsavoury. 22:28 And the
afflicted people thou wilt save: but thine eyes are upon the haughty, that thou
mayest bring them down. 22:29 For thou art my lamp, O LORD: and the
LORD will lighten my darkness. 22:30 For by thee I have run through a
troop: by my God have I leaped over a wall. 22:31 As for God, his way is
perfect; the word of the LORD is tried: he is a buckler to all them that trust
in him. 22:32 For who is God, save the LORD? and who is a rock, save our
God? 22:33 God is my strength and power: and he maketh my way perfect.
22:34 He maketh my feet like hinds' feet: and setteth me upon my high
places. 22:35 He teacheth my hands to war; so that a bow of steel is broken
by mine arms. 22:36 Thou hast also given me the shield of thy salvation: and
thy gentleness hath made me great. 22:37 Thou hast enlarged my steps
under me; so that my feet did not slip. 22:38 I have pursued mine enemies,
and destroyed them; and turned not again until I had consumed them.
22:39 And I have consumed them, and wounded them, that they could not
arise: yea, they are fallen under my feet. 22:40 For thou hast girded me with
strength to battle: them that rose up against me hast thou subdued under me.
22:41 Thou hast also given me the necks of mine enemies, that I might
destroy them that hate me. 22:42 They looked, but there was none to save;
even unto the LORD, but he answered them not. 22:43 Then did I beat
them as small as the dust of the earth, I did stamp them as the mire of the
street, and did spread them abroad. 22:44 Thou also hast delivered me from
the strivings of my people, thou hast kept me to be head of the heathen: a
people which I knew not shall serve me. 22:45 Strangers shall submit
themselves unto me: as soon as they hear, they shall be obedient unto me.
22:46 Strangers shall fade away, and they shall be afraid out of their close
places. 22:47 The LORD liveth; and blessed be my rock; and exalted be the
God of the rock of my salvation. 22:48 It is God that avengeth me, and that

bringeth down the people under me. 22:49 And that bringeth me forth from mine enemies: thou also hast lifted me up on high above them that rose up against me: thou hast delivered me from the violent man. 22:50 Therefore I will give thanks unto thee, O LORD, among the heathen, and I will sing praises unto thy name. 22:51 He is the tower of salvation for his king: and sheweth mercy to his anointed, unto David, and to his seed for evermore.

CHAPTER 23

23:1 Now these be the last words of David. David the son of Jesse said, and the man who was raised up on high, the anointed of the God of Jacob, and the sweet psalmist of Israel, said, 23:2 The Spirit of the LORD spake by me, and his word was in my tongue. 23:3 The God of Israel said, the Rock of Israel spake to me, He that ruleth over men must be just, ruling in the fear of God. 23:4 And he shall be as the light of the morning, when the sun riseth, even a morning without clouds; as the tender grass springing out of the earth by clear shining after rain. 23:5 Although my house be not so with God; yet he hath made with me an everlasting covenant, ordered in all things, and sure: for this is all my salvation, and all my desire, although he make it not to grow. 23:6 But the sons of Belial shall be all of them as thorns thrust away, because they cannot be taken with hands: 23:7 But the man that shall touch them must be fenced with iron and the staff of a spear; and they shall be utterly burned with fire in the same place. 23:8 These be the names of the mighty men whom David had: The Tachmonite that sat in the seat, chief among the captains; the same was Adino the Eznite: he lift up his spear against eight hundred, whom he slew at one time. 23:9 And after him was Eleazar the son of Dodo the Ahohite, one of the three mighty men with David, when they defied the Philistines that were there gathered together to battle, and the men of Israel were gone away: 23:10 He arose, and smote the Philistines until his hand was weary, and his hand clave unto the sword: and the LORD wrought a great victory that day; and the people returned after him only to spoil. 23:11 And after him was Shammah the son of Agee the Hararite. And the Philistines were gathered together into a troop, where was a piece of ground full of lentiles: and the people fled from the Philistines. 23:12 But he stood in the midst of the ground, and defended it, and slew the Philistines: and the LORD wrought a great victory. 23:13 And three of the thirty chief went down, and came to David in the harvest time unto the cave of Adullam: and the troop of the Philistines pitched in the valley of Rephaim. 23:14 And David was then in an hold, and the garrison of the Philistines was then in Bethlehem. 23:15 And David longed, and said, Oh that one would give me drink of the water of the well of Bethlehem, which is by the gate! 23:16 And the three mighty men brake through the host of the Philistines, and drew water out of the well of Bethlehem, that was by the gate, and took it, and brought it to David: nevertheless he would not drink thereof, but poured it out unto the LORD. 23:17 And he said, Be it far from me, O LORD, that I should do this: is not this the blood of the men that went in jeopardy of their lives? therefore he would not drink it. These things did these three mighty men. 23:18 And Abishai, the brother of Joab, the son of Zeruiah, was chief among three. And he lifted up his spear against three hundred, and slew them, and had the name among three. 23:19 Was he not most honourable of three? therefore he was their captain: howbeit he attained not unto the first three. 23:20 And Benaiah the son of Jehoiada, the son of a valiant man, of Kabzeel, who had done many acts, he slew two lionlike men of Moab: he went down also and slew a lion in the midst of a pit in time of snow: 23:21 And he slew an Egyptian, a goodly man: and the Egyptian had a spear in his hand; but he went down to him with a staff, and plucked the spear out of the Egyptian's hand, and slew him with his own spear. 23:22 These things did Benaiah the son of Jehoiada, and had the name among three mighty men. 23:23 He was more honourable than the thirty, but he attained not to the first three. And David set him over his guard. 23:24 Asahel the brother of Joab was one of the thirty; Elhanan the son of Dodo of Bethlehem, 23:25 Shammah the Harodite, Elika the Harodite, 23:26 Helez the Paltite, Ira the son of Ikkesh the Tekoite, 23:27 Abiezer the Anethothite, Mebunnai the Hushathite, 23:28 Zalmon the Ahohite, Maharai the Netophathite, 23:29 Heleb the son of Baanah, a

Netophathite, Ittai the son of Ribai out of Gibeah of the children of Benjamin, 23:30 Benaiah the Pirathonite, Hiddai of the brooks of Gaash, 23:31 Abialbon the Arbathite, Azmaveth the Barhumite, 23:32 Eliahba the Shaalbonite, of the sons of Jashen, Jonathan, 23:33 Shammah the Hararite, Ahiam the son of Sharar the Hararite, 23:34 Eliphelet the son of Ahasbai, the son of the Maachathite, Eliam the son of Ahithophel the Gilonite, 23:35 Hezrai the Carmelite, Paarai the Arbite, 23:36 Igal the son of Nathan of Zobah, Bani the Gadite, 23:37 Zelek the Ammonite, Nahari the Beerothite, armourbearer to Joab the son of Zeruiah, 23:38 Ira an Ithrite, Gareb an Ithrite, 23:39 Uriah the Hittite: thirty and seven in all.

CHAPTER 24

24:1 And again the anger of the LORD was kindled against Israel, and he moved David against them to say, Go, number Israel and Judah. 24:2 For the king said to Joab the captain of the host, which was with him, Go now through all the tribes of Israel, from Dan even to Beersheba, and number ye the people, that I may know the number of the people. 24:3 And Joab said unto the king, Now the LORD thy God add unto the people, how many soever they be, an hundredfold, and that the eyes of my lord the king may see it: but why doth my lord the king delight in this thing? 24:4 Notwithstanding the king's word prevailed against Joab, and against the captains of the host. And Joab and the captains of the host went out from the presence of the king, to number the people of Israel. 24:5 And they passed over Jordan, and pitched in Aroer, on the right side of the city that lieth in the midst of the river of Gad, and toward Jazer: 24:6 Then they came to Gilead, and to the land of Tahtimhodshi; and they came to Danjaan, and about to Zidon, 24:7 And came to the strong hold of Tyre, and to all the cities of the Hivites, and of the Canaanites: and they went out to the south of Judah, even to Beersheba. 24:8 So when they had gone through all the land, they came to Jerusalem at the end of nine months and twenty days. 24:9 And Joab gave up the sum of the number of the people unto the king: and there were in Israel eight hundred thousand valiant men that drew the sword; and the men of Judah were five hundred thousand men. 24:10 And David's heart smote him after that he had numbered the people. And David said unto the LORD, I have sinned greatly in that I have done: and now, I beseech thee, O LORD, take away the iniquity of thy servant; for I have done very foolishly. 24:11 For when David was up in the morning, the word of the LORD came unto the prophet Gad, David's seer, saying, 24:12 Go and say unto David, Thus saith the LORD, I offer thee three things; choose thee one of them, that I may do it unto thee. 24:13 So Gad came to David, and told him, and said unto him, Shall seven years of famine come unto thee in thy land? or wilt thou flee three months before thine enemies, while they pursue thee? or that there be three days' pestilence in thy land? now advise, and see what answer I shall return to him that sent me. 24:14 And David said unto Gad, I am in a great strait: let us fall now into the hand of the LORD; for his mercies are great: and let me not fall into the hand of man. 24:15 So the LORD sent a pestilence upon Israel from the morning even to the time appointed: and there died of the people from Dan even to Beersheba seventy thousand men. 24:16 And when the angel stretched out his hand upon Jerusalem to destroy it, the LORD repented him of the evil, and said to the angel that destroyed the people, It is enough: stay now thine hand. And the angel of the LORD was by the threshingplace of Araunah the Jebusite. 24:17 And David spake unto the LORD when he saw the angel that smote the people, and said, Lo, I have sinned, and I have done wickedly: but these sheep, what have they done? let thine hand, I pray thee, be against me, and against my father's house. 24:18 And Gad came that day to David, and said unto him, Go up, rear an altar unto the LORD in the threshingfloor of Araunah the Jebusite. 24:19 And David, according to the saying of Gad, went up as the LORD commanded. 24:20 And Araunah looked, and saw the king and his servants coming on toward him: and Araunah went out, and bowed himself before the king on his face upon the ground. 24:21 And Araunah said, Wherefore is my lord the king come to his servant? And David said, To buy the threshingfloor of thee, to build an altar unto the LORD, that the plague may be stayed from the people. 24:22 And Araunah said

unto David, Let my lord the king take and offer up what seemeth good unto
him: behold, here be oxen for burnt sacrifice, and threshing instruments and
other instruments of the oxen for wood. 24:23 All these things did Araunah,
as a king, give unto the king. And Araunah said unto the king, The LORD
thy God accept thee. 24:24 And the king said unto Araunah, Nay; but I will
surely buy it of thee at a price: neither will I offer burnt offerings unto the
LORD my God of that which doth cost me nothing. So David bought the
threshingfloor and the oxen for fifty shekels of silver. 24:25 And David built
there an altar unto the LORD, and offered burnt offerings and peace
offerings. So the LORD was intreated for the land, and the plague was stayed
from Israel.

Other books in this series available from Sublime Books.

The Old Testament

978-1-5154-4078-9 The First Book of Moses: Genesis
978-1-5154-4079-6 The Second Book of Moses: Exodus
978-1-5154-4080-2 L The Third Book of Moses: Leviticus
978-1-5154-4081-9 The Fourth Book of Moses: Numbers
978-1-5154-4082-6 The Fifth Book of Moses: Deuteronomy
978-1-5154-4083-3 The Book of Joshua
978-1-5154-4084-0 The Book of Judges
978-1-5154-4085-7 The Book of Ruth
978-1-5154-4086-4 The First Book of Samuel
978-1-5154-4087-1 The Second Book of Samuel
978-1-5154-4088-8 The First Book of the Kings
978-1-5154-4089-5 The Second Book of the Kings
978-1-5154-4090-1 The First Book of the Chronicles
978-1-5154-4091-8 The Second Book of the Chronicles
978-1-5154-4092-5 The Book of Ezra
978-1-5154-4093-2 The Book of Nehemiah
978-1-5154-4094-9 The Book of Esther
978-1-5154-4095-6 The Book of Job
978-1-5154-4096-3 The Book of Psalms
978-1-5154-4097-0 The Proverbs
978-1-5154-4098-7 The Book of Ecclesiastes
978-1-5154-4099-4 The Song of Solomon
978-1-5154-4100-7 The Book of the Prophet Isaiah
978-1-5154-4101-4 The Book of the Prophet Jeremiah
978-1-5154-4102-1 The Lamentations of Jeremiah
978-1-5154-4103-8 The Book of the Prophet Ezekiel
978-1-5154-4104-5 The Book of Daniel
978-1-5154-4105-2 The Book of Hosea
978-1-5154-4106-9 The Book of Joel
978-1-5154-4107-6 The Book of Amos

978-1-5154-4108-3 The Book of Obadiah
978-1-5154-4109-0 The Book of Jonah
978-1-5154-4110-6 The Book of Micah
978-1-5154-4111-3 The Book of Nahum
978-1-5154-4112-0 The Book of Habakkuk
978-1-5154-4113-7 The Book of Zephaniah
978-1-5154-4114-4 The Book of Haggai
978-1-5154-4115-1 The Book of Zechariah
978-1-5154-4116-8 The Book of Malachi

The New Testament

978-1-5154-4117-5 The Gospel According to Saint Matthew
978-1-5154-4118-2 The Gospel According to Saint Mark
978-1-5154-4119-9 The Gospel According to Saint Luke
978-1-5154-4120-5 The Gospel According to Saint John
978-1-5154-4121-2 The Acts of the Apostles
978-1-5154-4122-9 The Epistle of Paul the Apostle to the Romans
978-1-5154-4123-6 The First Epistle of Paul the Apostle to the Corinthians
978-1-5154-4124-3 The Second Epistle of Paul the Apostle to the Corinthians
978-1-5154-4125-0 The Epistle of Paul the Apostle to the Galatians
978-1-5154-4126-7 The Epistle of Paul the Apostle to the Ephesians
978-1-5154-4127-4 The Epistle of Paul the Apostle to the Philippians
978-1-5154-4128-1 The Epistle of Paul the Apostle to the Colossians
978-1-5154-4129-8 The First Epistle of Paul the Apostle to the Thessalonians
978-1-5154-4130-4 The Second Epistle of Paul the Apostle to the Thessalonians
978-1-5154-4131-1 The First Epistle of Paul the Apostle to Timothy
978-1-5154-4132-8 The Second Epistle of Paul the Apostle to Timothy
978-1-5154-4133-5 The Epistle of Paul the Apostle to Titus
978-1-5154-4134-2 The Epistle of Paul the Apostle to Philemon
978-1-5154-4135-9 The Epistle of Paul the Apostle to the Hebrews
978-1-5154-4136-6 The General Epistle of James

978-1-5154-4137-3 The First Epistle General of Peter
978-1-5154-4138-0 The Second General Epistle of Peter
978-1-5154-4139-7 The First Epistle General of John
978-1-5154-4140-3 The Second Epistle General of John
978-1-5154-4141-0 The Third Epistle General of John
978-1-5154-4142-7 The General Epistle of Jude
978-1-5154-4143-4 The Revelation of Saint John the Devine

www.ingramcontent.com/pod-product-compliance
Lightning Source LLC
Chambersburg PA
CBHW030415310726
48979CB00002B/428

* 9 7 9 8 8 8 0 9 1 0 9 7 7 *